This
Treasure Cove Story
belongs to

FINDING NEMO

A CENTUM BOOK 9 978-1-912396-09-2
Published in Great Britain by Centum Books Ltd.
This edition published 2018. 1 3 5 7 9 10 8 6 4 2

Centum Books Ltd, 20 Devon Square, Newton Abbot,
Devon, TQ12 2HR, UK.

www.centumbooksltd.co.uk | books@centumbooksltd.co.uk
CENTUM BOOKS Limited Reg.No. 07641486.

A CIP catalogue record for this book is available
from the British Library.

Printed in China.

centum

A Treasure Cove Story

Adapted by Victoria Saxon

Illustrated by Scott Tilley

Designed by Disney's Global Design Group

Now, most of you who are reading this book probably live above the sea…

…but others live underwater.

Nemo and his father, Marlin, lived underwater. They were clownfish.

Because they were clownfish, they were small. But other fish were big!

Marlin was scared of the big fish, so he always kept Nemo close to him, tucked safely inside their little home.

But today was Nemo's first day of school!
He was very excited. On the way there he saw…

a spotted fish...

…and a striped fish.

He saw grumpy fish…

…and
H A P P Y fish.

Mr Ray, the science teacher, took
Nemo's class on a school trip. Nemo
and his friends sneaked away and
swam to the really deep water.
Marlin chased after Nemo and
scolded him! Nemo was angry
that his father had embarrassed
him in front of his new friends…

...so he swam

...and swam

...and swam

way up to the surface
of the ocean until he
touched a boat!

Then Nemo got caught!
'Daddy!' cried Nemo.
'Nemo!' cried Marlin.

Nemo was taken away in the boat. Marlin
tried to save his son, but the boat sped away
so fast it soon disappeared. Nemo was gone.
But Marlin would not give up. The only thing
on his mind now was finding Nemo.

Looking for help, Marlin swam into all sorts
of fish. They pushed him and shoved him. They
bumped into him. Soon Marlin was knocked aside.

One friendly fish named Dory swam down to see if Marlin was okay. She was a little bit silly, and she couldn't remember very much, but she was happy to help Marlin!

Together, Dory and Marlin met a shark. Marlin was scared! But Dory thought it was very nice of the shark to invite them to a party.

The party was for sharks who were trying not to eat fish. Luckily, they did not eat Marlin and Dory.

Marlin kept searching for
Nemo. He and Dory found
a scuba mask that belonged to
the diver who had taken Nemo.
They swam down into a very
deep, dark place to get it.

Then they saw a light.

The light was attached to a mean anglerfish! But it helped Dory read an address written on the mask. Then the two friends swam away before the anglerfish could eat them! Now Marlin knew where to find Nemo: 42 Wallaby Way, Sydney. Dory was so excited that she repeated the address over and over… and over.

Next Marlin and Dory met some moonfish.
The moonfish made funny shapes.

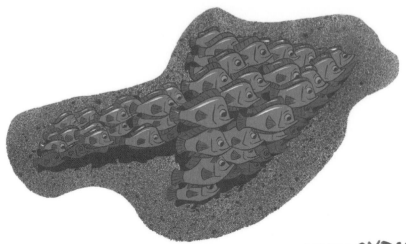

They pointed towards 42 WALLABY WAY, SYDNEY.

Some friendly turtles
gave Marlin and Dory a ride.

Marlin told the
story of his search
for Nemo, and the
news spread across
the ocean!

Even Nemo heard about it at 42 Wallaby Way,
Sydney. He was very excited! He wanted to
escape from the fish tank where he was trapped.

Nemo's new friends were excited, too.
The little clownfish was bursting with pride.
He had the bravest dad in the sea!

Then a whale swallowed Marlin and Dory!
Dory told Marlin he didn't need to worry.
    And she was right. The whale took them
as close as he could get to 42 Wallaby Way,
Sydney. In fact, he took them all the way to
Sydney Harbour!

At last a pelican named
Nigel helped Marlin and
Dory go straight to 42 Wallaby
Way, Sydney. But it was
too late. A little girl had
grabbed Nemo. Marlin
couldn't save him!

Marlin was sad. He thought he would never see his son again.

But Nemo had escaped! Dory found him.

Father and son were overjoyed.

And when they finally returned home, both Nemo and Marlin were heroes.

Treasure Cove Stories

Book list may be subject to change.

An ongoing series to collect and enjoy!